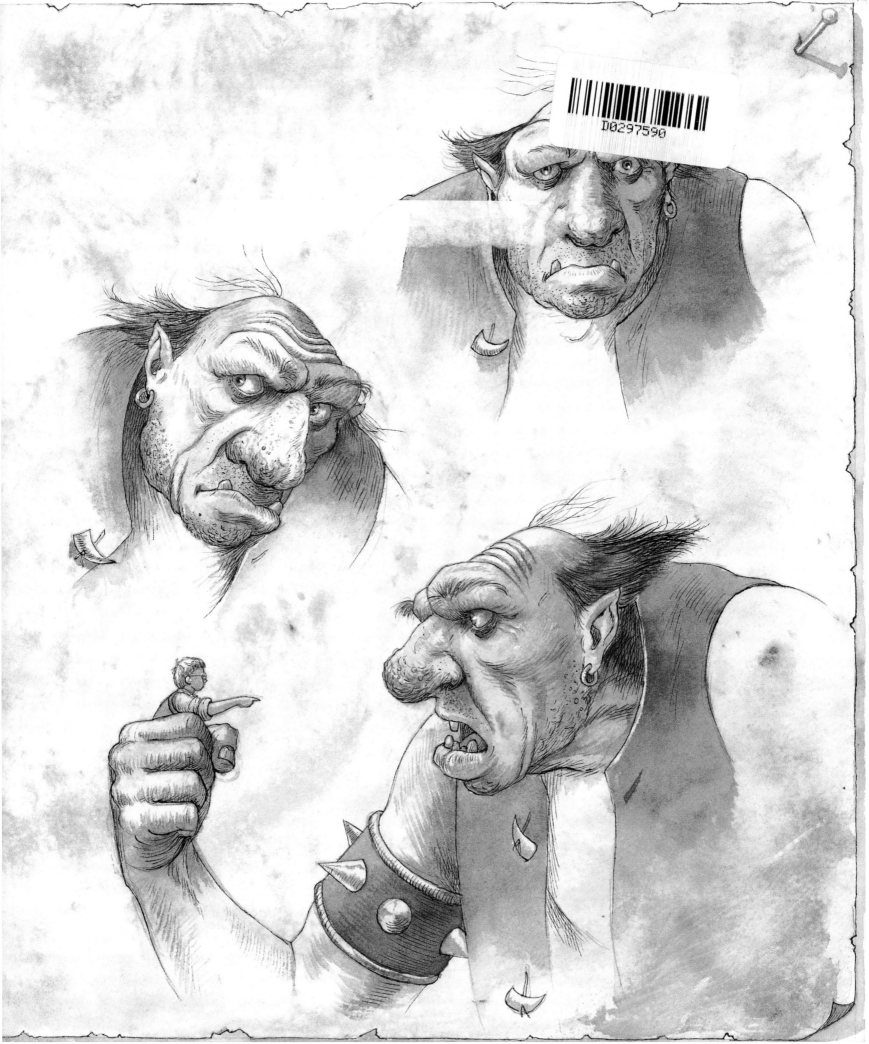

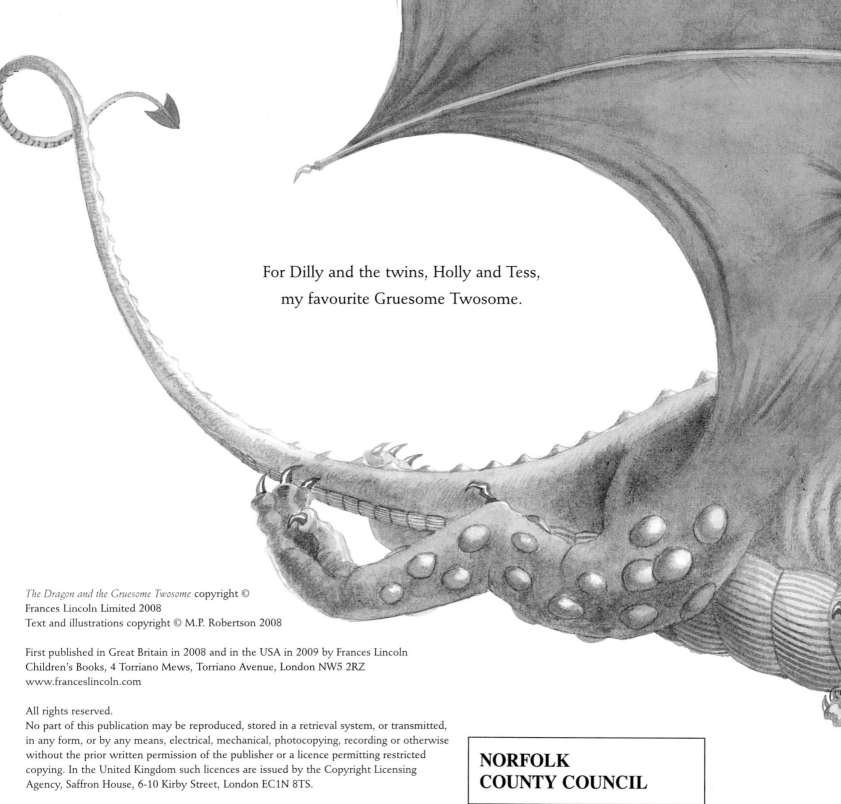

For Dilly and the twins, Holly and Tess,
my favourite Gruesome Twosome.

The Dragon and the Gruesome Twosome copyright ©
Frances Lincoln Limited 2008
Text and illustrations copyright © M.P. Robertson 2008

First published in Great Britain in 2008 and in the USA in 2009 by Frances Lincoln
Children's Books, 4 Torriano Mews, Torriano Avenue, London NW5 2RZ
www.franceslincoln.com

British Library Cataloguing in Publication Data available on request

ISBN: 978-1-84507-763-1

The illustrations for this book are in watercolour.

Set in StempelSchneidler

Printed in China

9 8 7 6 5 4 3 2 1

Read more about George's adventures on the author's website: **www.mprobertson.com**

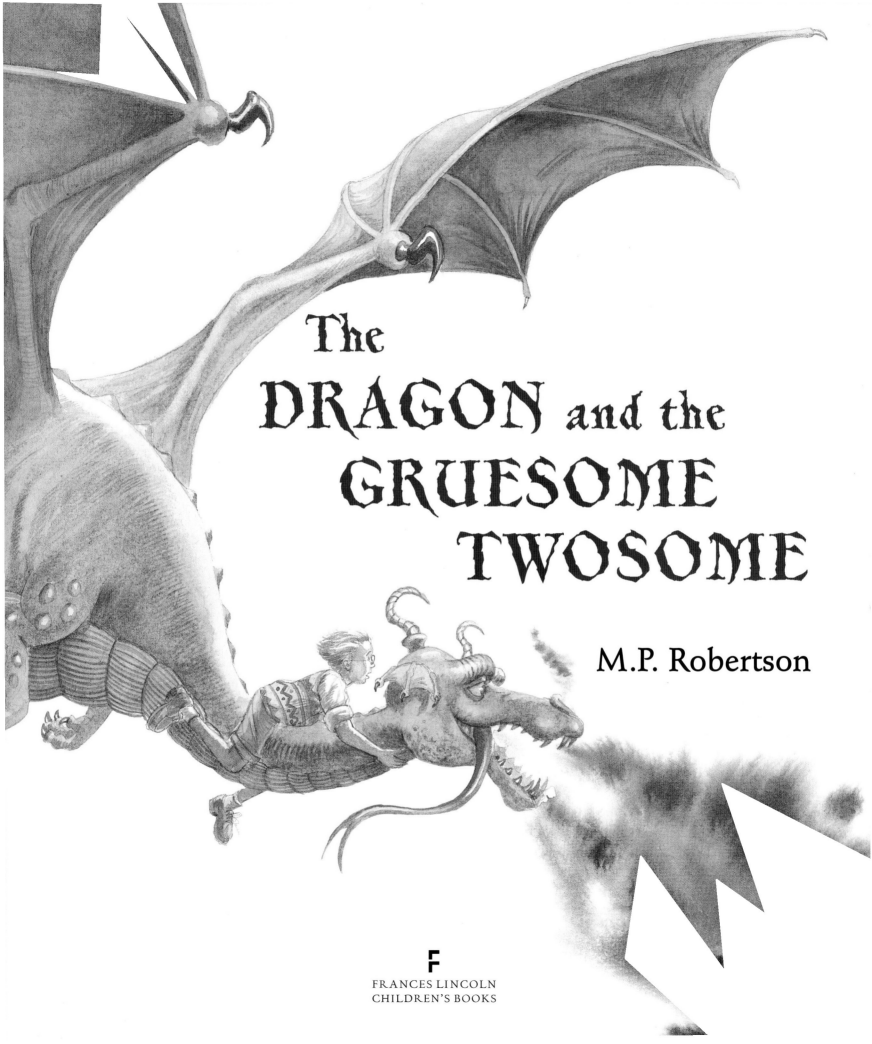

The DRAGON and the GRUESOME TWOSOME

M.P. Robertson

F

FRANCES LINCOLN
CHILDREN'S BOOKS

George had a problem. His mother's favourite chicken had taken to roosting in a tree, and every time she laid an egg it smashed on the ground.

Just then the leaves of the tree began to rustle. George heard a beating of wings and his dragon swooped down from the sky. The chicken was so flustered she laid an egg. George caught it – on his head!

George knew that an adventure was about to begin. He clambered on the dragon's back and they soared into the sky.

Round and round the world they sped until they came to a land where knights were bold, and carried big shiny swords to prove it.

There were no crops in the fields, trees had been ripped from the ground and where there should have been animals there was nothing but bones.

Then George saw a castle in the distance but, as they drew nearer, he could see that its turrets and walls had been smashed.

Something had been attacking the castle.

The dragon hovered above the castle wall and George used the dragon's tail like a rope to lower himself down.

There was a market in the street but no one in this market was happy. There were only a handful of stalls and all they had for sale were a few mouldy mango-wurzels and rats.

George spotted a notice pinned to a post.

WANTED

GOBBLEDEGOOK AND BALDERDASH

Anyone who can rid the land
of this gruesome twosome,
will be rewarded with
half my kingdom.

The King

As George looked at the notice, an old woman sidled up to him.

"Buy a nice juicy rat, my dear?" she croaked.

"No thanks," replied George. "I'm not that hungry."

"Not 'ungry? Everyone from these parts is 'ungry," she said.

She pointed at the notice. "Fancy your chances do you? Knights from seven kingdoms have tried. Some were big and bold. Others were brave and shiny. But when faced with the terrible twins, their boldness and bravery disappeared."

The old woman shook her head.

"Even all the King's 'orses and all the King's men were no match for these monsters. Arrows and spears just bounced off their leathery skin. They're a right gruesome twosome – double trouble! They can eat more in a day than an army will eat in a year and all that's left is rats and stinkin' turnips! But they won't stop when they 'ave eaten all our food – they'll want to eat us as well! So far the castle walls have kept 'em out – but it is only a matter of time."

George knew he must help. He didn't carry a big
sword but he had his wit, which was as sharp as a
tailor's needle. And he had his dragon!

He found a coil of rope and whistled for his dragon.
They followed the trail of devastation until they found
the trolls gobbling up a herd of sheep – wool and all.

George and the dragon hid in a wood. Eventually
Balderdash lay down and it wasn't long before
his snores rumbled like thunder. George whispered
his plan to the dragon.

The dragon flew out of the woods and began
to taunt Gobbledegook. He flicked him with his tail
and set his pants alight with a fiery blast. The troll
was furious. He chased the dragon over the fields,
far away from his sleeping brother.

When Gobbledegook and the dragon were out of sight,
George gave a polite cough, but Balderdash's snores
rumbled on. So George jumped up and down
on the troll's warty nose.

The troll's huge eye snapped open and he snatched
George up in his fist.

"Why aren't you scared?" bellowed Balderdash.

"You're not scary," laughed George.

"I am scary. I'm big and smelly and scary.
My mummy told me that."

"Well, you are big and smelly," said George,
"but you are not scary. I have heard that there is a very
scary troll called Gobbledegook. He has been
telling everyone that his brother,
Balderdash, is a bit of a wimp."

"WIMP! I'll show him who's a
wimp!" roared the troll.

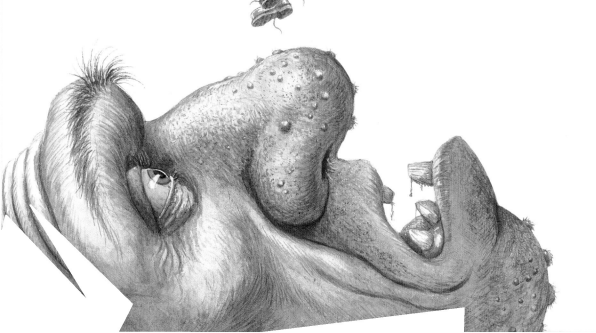

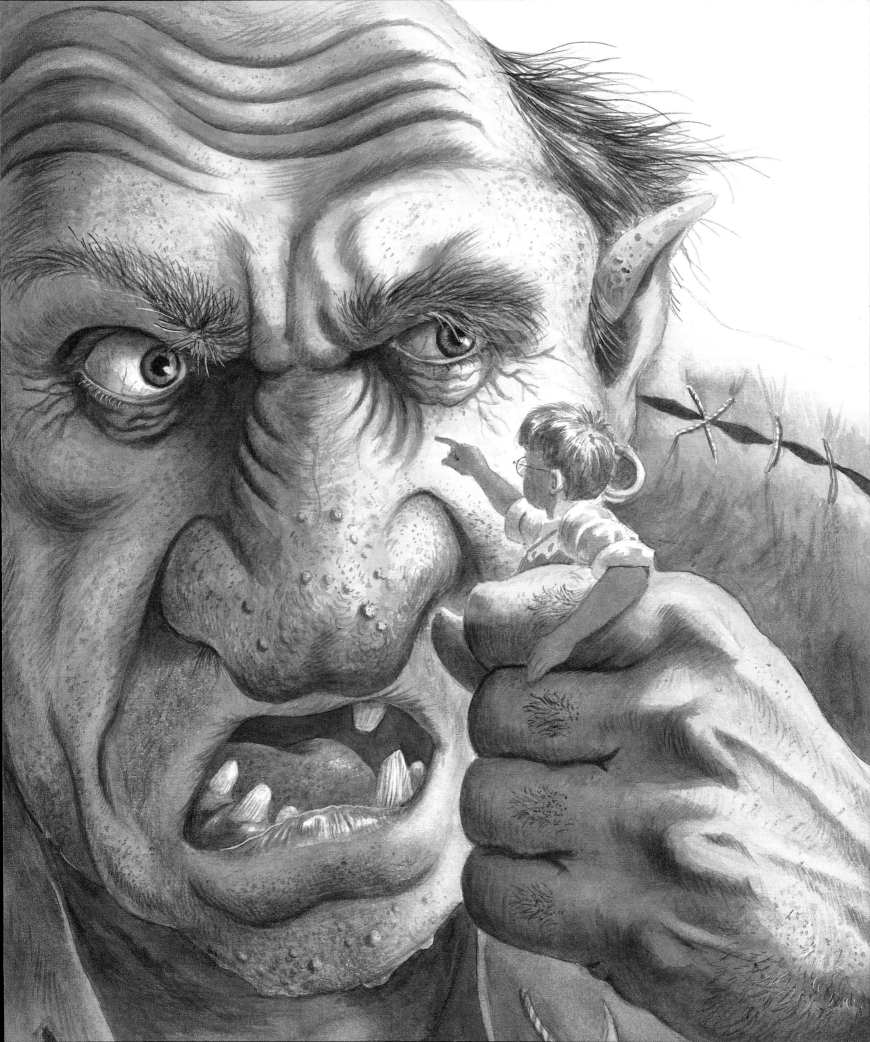

Just at that moment Goobledegook returned,
looking singed and very angry. Balderdash gave
a fierce yell and charged at his brother.

With an almighty punch he sent Gobbledegook
crashing to the ground.

George watched as the brothers beat each other black and blue.

All through the night they fought. The people in the castle quivered in their beds as the trolls' bellows roared throughout the kingdom. By morning the twins were exhausted with not an ounce of fight left in them.

George hung a loop of rope around the trolls' necks. Then he headed for the palace, with the trolls following behind, as meek as two kittens.

George led the trolls through the town,
and the King came to greet him.

"You have succeeded where my knights have
failed," said the King. "Half my kingdom is yours."

"That's very kind," said George. "But it's hard
enough looking after a few chickens. I don't think
I could manage half a kingdom."

"But you must have a reward," said the King.

"Actually there is one thing…"
said George.

As George and his dragon flew into the sky, the people from the castle cheered. In George's hand there was a bulging sack.

Soon George could see his own kingdom below. The chicken coop was his castle, the chickens were his subjects and the dragon was his steed...

...what more could a boy possibly want?